for Rebecca and Bruno

and for e.

TERTIUS and PLINY

WRITTEN BY Ben Frankel

ILLUSTRATED BY Emma Chichester Clark

Gulliver Books
Harcourt Brace Jovanovich, Publishers
SAN DIEGO   NEW YORK   LONDON

First published 1992 by Methuen Children's Books
First U.S. edition 1992

Library of Congress Cataloging-in-Publication Data
Frankel, Ben.
Tertius and Pliny/by Ben Frankel; illustrated by Emma
Chichester Clark.
p. cm.
"Gulliver books."
Summary: Tertius the stuffed dog plans and executes the rescue of
his friend Pliny, a toy monkey, from a shop.
ISBN 0-15-200604-4
[1. Toys—Fiction. 2. Dogs—Fiction. 3. Monkeys—Fiction.]
I. Chichester Clark, Emma, ill. II. Title.
PZ7.F8529Te   1992
[E]—dc20   91-24145

Printed in Hong Kong

A B C D E

For almost as long as they could remember, Tertius and Pliny had lived in the small cubbyhole that served as Mrs. Kay's shop. The shop was around the corner and upstairs in a building that sold old furniture and the things some people call antiques.

Tertius didn't know how old he was—he felt young and alert, and he wanted to escape from the shop. Pliny dimly remembered a distant green jungle where he would swing from tree to tree, but now, because he had only one glass eye and knew no better, he enjoyed life in Mrs. Kay's dark, cozy shop.

Mrs. Kay was nice enough, but it never occurred to her to find another
eye for Pliny from the jar she kept on her desk. Few people were tempted
to visit her cubbyhole filled with necklaces, glass vases, and toy animals.
Tertius longed for someone to buy him, but the grown-ups who collected
toy animals were a bit peculiar.

One day two children named Bruno and Rebecca came into the shop.
Their Uncle Max had been dragging them into antique shops all afternoon,
and they were grumpy. Suddenly Bruno saw Tertius, Tertius saw Rebecca,
and both children begged their uncle to buy him for them.

Uncle Max said Tertius was too expensive and began to leave. Tertius tried to change Uncle Max's mind by licking his hand. Uncle Max knew toy animals didn't have tongues. Surprised, he found himself buying the funny little dog. Bruno and Rebecca were delighted.

Pliny sadly waved farewell. Now he supposed there would be more space on the shelf, especially for his tail, but he realized there would be no one to joke with about Mrs. Kay or to applaud his acrobatics as he swung among the glass vases without breaking them.

Tertius soon settled down in his new home, but he did not forget his old friend. Among Bruno's and Rebecca's toys was a daredevil red airplane named Baron Hendrik von Krug. Baron von Krug found the children's other toys tame and dull, so he was delighted to meet Tertius, who seemed curious to see life in the world outside.

Sometimes at night the Baron took Tertius flying. One night they flew
out of the garden, over the city, and Tertius spotted the building where

Mrs. Kay's shop was. It was then that Tertius told the Baron about his friend, Pliny, and they decided to rescue him together.

Late one afternoon, while Rebecca and Bruno were at school, the
Baron flew with Tertius to the shop. They soared high over the rooftops.

As they dipped down toward the street they almost collided with a straggly line of school children. A naughty boy tried to grab Tertius by the leg, but fortunately Tertius had some sharp teeth left, and he nipped the boy's wrist lightly.

The Baron swooped up, and soon they were above the children and their startled teacher.

It was a great escape!

The two adventurers'
hearts were still thumping
when they reached the
building. Luckily there
was no one in sight, so the
Baron flew upstairs and, lo
and behold, there was the
shop with Mrs. Kay inside.
But there was no sign of
Pliny.

Tertius crept inside the shop and whispered his friend's name. Out from the darkest corner Pliny appeared, his one eye shining in amazement as he swung down from the shelf.

While the Baron distracted Mrs. Kay by weaving and zooming above her desk, Tertius and Pliny raced out the door.

They jumped onto the Baron's wings and quickly flew out of the shop
and back the way they had come.

By now it was dark, and Pliny was a bit nervous. It was the first time he had been outside in a long while. But Tertius reassured him that it would soon be light again.

Baron von Krug said he preferred the dark because he could fly without being seen and could use his special night-flying navigational skills. Just then, billowing smoke from a chimney engulfed the three, almost choking them.

Although the Baron
was protected by his
goggles, he nearly crashed
into some scaffolding—
grazing his left wing.
Tertius and Pliny hung on
bravely, trusting the
Baron. Pliny was extra
careful to keep his long tail
away from the dangerous
propeller.

Soon they swooped through the playroom window, safe at last. The Baron hadn't enjoyed himseif so much in ages and was pleased that the rescue had been a success.

The next morning the children couldn't understand where Pliny had suddenly appeared from, but they were very pleased to meet him. Bruno was surprised to see the Baron's grazed wing and carefully mended it. Rebecca found a shiny glass button that matched Pliny's one eye very well. She gently sewed it on without hurting him.

Now Pliny could see with two eyes, and he happily began the first day of his new life. Tertius was delighted to be with his old companion again. And as for the Baron, he was looking forward to having more adventures with his fearless friends.